MW00744047

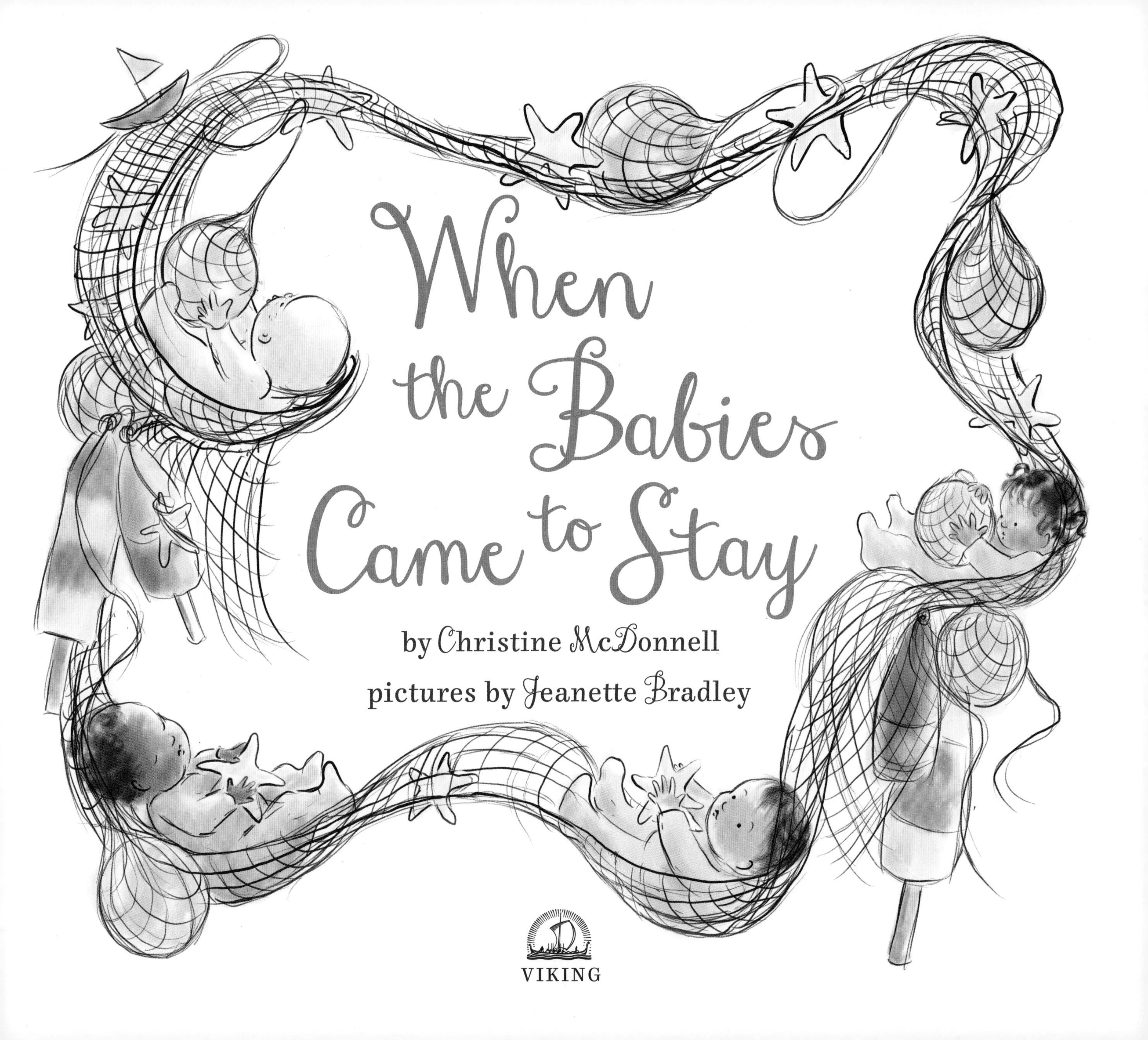

When the Babies Came to Stay

by Christine McDonnell

pictures by Jeanette Bradley

VIKING

For Henry.
—C.M.

For librarians everywhere—thanks for usually knowing the answers.
—J.B.

With thanks to Agatha Christie, Bram Stoker, Charles Dickens, and Dorothy L. Sayers for lending their names.

VIKING
An imprint of Penguin Random House LLC, New York

First published in the United States of America by Viking,
an imprint of Penguin Random House LLC, 2020

Visit us online at penguinrandomhouse.com

LIBRARY OF CONGRESS CATALOGING-IN-PUBLICATION DATA IS AVAILABLE
ISBN 9781984835451

Manufactured in China   Set in Cosmiqua Com

10 9 8 7 6 5 4 3 2 1

The artwork for this book was digitally painted using Procreate for iPad.

The first arrived on the mail plane.

The harbormaster opened the canvas bag.
Inside was a squalling, red-faced baby.

The next two came on the ferry,
tucked in a carryall left on a seat.
The ferryman carried the babies ashore.

The fisherman found the fourth on the pier,
asleep on a pile of nets,
smelling faintly of mackerel.

Four little babies on one small island.
Where did they come from?
Where did they belong?

"Will they ever be quiet?" asked the fisherman.
"What do they eat?" asked the ferryman.
"What should we do with them?" asked the harbormaster.

"Return them to the mainland,"
bellowed the mayor.

"But should we?" the librarian asked.
She usually knew the answers to questions.

She read the notes on their blankets aloud:
"'Please keep this baby safe,'
'Please raise these babies well,'
and 'Please give my child shelter.'"

The librarian smiled at the babies . . .
"Here is where they're meant to live,
on our safe little island."

"I can't take them," the ferryman said.
"I've too many small fry at home."
"I'm at sea every day," said the fisherman.
"I'm busy with boats," said the harbormaster.
"My work's too important," said the mayor,
his chest puffed out like a gull's.

"Then I'll do it myself," the librarian said.

The librarian lived above the library
with treetops in her windows.
She slept in the attic.
The skylight above her bed
showed the moon and stars at night
and the sun woke her in the morning.

Where would the babies fit?

The librarian emptied the storeroom.
She painted the walls and polished the floor.

The fisherman made cribs from
lobster traps.

The harbormaster sewed sails into coverlets.

The ferryman strung nets in the windows.

The mayor gave his approval.

FIELD GUIDE TO THE NORTH AMERICAN MERMAID
LOCAL ISLAND AUTHORS
Sail Away
1001 FISH RECIPES

“What shall we call them?” the librarian asked.
“Fred and Ned and Ed and Ted?” the ferryman suggested.
“Two are girls,“ the librarian reminded him.
“Peg and Meg?” the fisherman said.
“Name one after me,” said the mayor. (Murgatroyd was his name.)
The librarian looked at the shelves. She knew what to do.
She named them alphabetically in order of arrival.
Agatha who came by air,
Bram and Charles who arrived on the ferry,
Dorothy who napped on a pile of nets.
And their last name? Book, of course.

When she was in a hurry
she called them A, B, C, and D.
Quite often she simply called them Books.

"Supper's ready, Books!"

"Bath time for Books."

"All Books in bed."
"Time for books for my Books."

Agatha was the roundest.
She was the first to stand.

Bram was the tallest.
He was the first to walk.

Charles was loud as clamoring gulls.
He was the first to talk.
His first word? *Book*, of course.

And Dorothy was quiet as fog.
She loved to laugh.

A year went by, and then another.
The babies belonged to the island.

The fisherman sang them chanties.

The ferryman let them sound his horn.

The harbormaster tied them each a knot,

and the mayor spun them around in his chair.

The fisherman taught them to cast from the pier.

The ferryman showed them charts of the sea.

The harbormaster taught them to recognize birds:
sandpipers, plovers, and terns.

The librarian taught them to read,
of course.

The Books grew up on the island.
They knew the marshes, inlets, coves, and flats,
the scent of low tide and the crunch of sand,
the taste of sea salt on their lips,
the song of the wind on stormy nights
as they read beside the bright red stove.

The other island children were curious.
“Why do you live in the library?” they asked.
“Why don’t you look alike?” and
“Where are you really from?”

The Books brought the questions to the librarian,
who usually knew the answers.

The librarian gathered them in the circle of her arms.
"Some questions don't have answers," she said.
"Some mysteries are never solved."
She read them the notes that came pinned to their blankets.
"Your parents sent you here with love.
They wanted you to be safe.
The library is our home.
Families don't always look alike, you know, and where
we're going is more important than where we came from."
"Where are we going?" the Books asked.
"To bed!" she said.

That night she told them their favorite story:
how Agatha came by air,
Charles and Bram arrived on the ferry,
and Dorothy appeared on a pile of nets,
the best catch of the day.
"Your last name is Book," she reminded them.
"And that's your name, too!" they said.
"Yes, I am Eleanor Book," she said as she
tucked them in.
"So we are A, B, C, D, and E."

A, B, C, D, and E were a set of Books.
The library was where they lived,
and the island was where they belonged.